A Giant First-Start Reader

This easy reader contains only 31 different words, repeated often to help the young reader develop word recognition and interest in reading.

Basic word list for *Mud Pies*

all	help	of
apple	I	pies
are	ice	sister
best	lemon	small
big	like	some
brother	made	the
cherry	make	them
come	makes	too
cream	mother	whipped
father	mud	with
	my	

Mud Pies

Written by Judith Grey

Illustrated by Deborah Sims

Troll Associates

Library of Congress Cataloging in Publication Data

Grey, Judith.
    Mud pies.

    Summary: A child talks about a variety of pies,
including mud pies.
    [1. Pies—Fiction]   I. Sims, Deborah.   II. Title.
PZ7.G868Mu   [E]   81-4042
ISBN 0-89375-541-9   AACR2
ISBN 0-89375-542-7 (pbk.)

Copyright © 1981 by Troll Associates, Mahwah, New Jersey

All rights reserved. No part of this book may be used or
reproduced in any manner whatsoever without written
permission from the publisher.
Printed in the United States of America.
10   9   8   7   6   5   4   3   2

Some pies are made of mud.

Some pies are made of apple.

Some pies are made of cherry.

Some pies are made of lemon.

Some pies come with ice cream.

Some pies come with whipped cream.

Some pies are big.

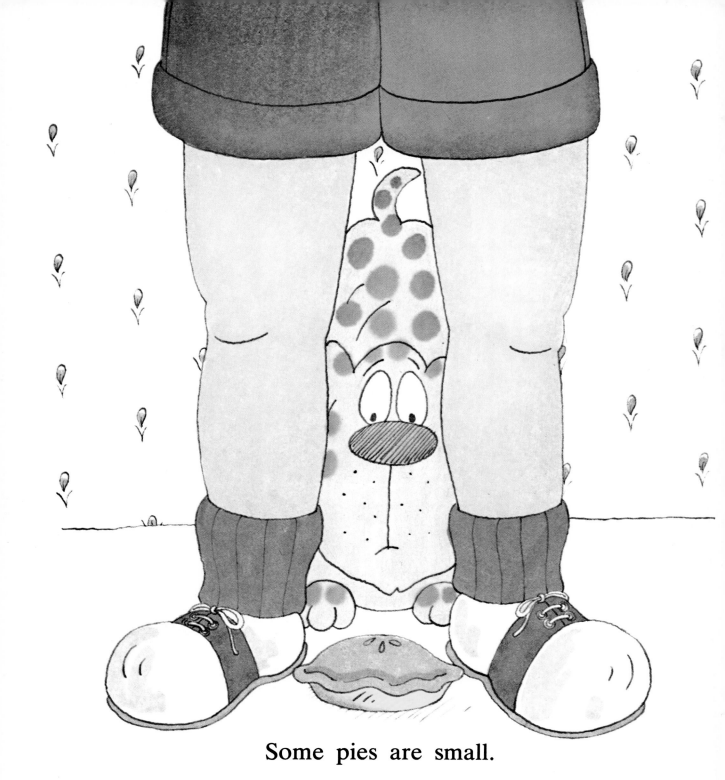

Some pies are small.

I like pies.

I like them all.

I like apple pies.

I like cherry pies.

I like lemon pies.

I like pies with ice cream.

I like pies with whipped cream.

I like pies!

My mother makes cherry pies.

My father makes apple pies.

My sister makes pies with whipped cream.

My brother makes pies with ice cream.

I make pies, too.

I help my mother make cherry pies.

I help my father make apple pies.

I help my sister make pies with whipped cream.

I help my brother make pies with ice cream.

The pies I like best of all—

the pies I make best of all—

are mud pies!